Charlo and the Lemonade Stand

The Number Investigators 2

Martin Tiller

ISBN: 978-0-9996879-2-5

For Rachel

Thanks to Jenifer Ring for her help with the book and her continued support.

To all students who enjoy numbers and enjoy math.

Chapters

Chapter 1 Mom Calls Me Charlotte Morgan When I am in Trouble

My name is Charlotte Morgan, and I am good with numbers. My friends like numbers as well. Sally, Marcus, Aaron, and I all make up The Number Investigators. We hold our meetings in my awesome tree house. We all competed in our school's annual math bee. I was the runner-up for the whole school. A fifth grader named Sanjey won. He is going to go to a county-wide math bee. My dad teaches math at the high school. So, he is really good at numbers, too. I guess that's where I get it from. Today is Saturday and it is 73 degrees Fahrenheit, or 23 degrees in Celsius, outside.

"Charlotte Morgan! Charlie chewed up one of my shoes!" my mom shouted from her bedroom. Mom calls me Charlotte Morgan when I am in trouble.

Charlie is my new Labrador puppy. He is about ten weeks old. And he likes to chew on things.

I zoomed up the seventeen steps to the second floor. Charlie may be in as much trouble as I am.

"Yes. Mom, what happened?" I asked. My mom showed me the shoe. Charlie was following her. Maybe he thought she was going to drop the shoe and let him finish eating it. "I'm sorry."

"That pair of shoes was seventy-five dollars." Mom pointed out of her room, "Take him for a walk and work with him."

"Yes, ma'am," I picked Charlie up and took him to the kitchen. I put his yellow leash on him. His tail wagged so hard it made a flapping noise has it hit my leg and the leg of the kitchen chair. I picked up a yellow tennis ball and took him outside.

"Come on boy," I said as I gently led him on the leash. I led him to the driveway and then to the street. "Let's get some of that energy out of you!" I spoke in a high-pitched voice. Charlie jumped up and down when I spoke in that voice.

It was Saturday, so, there were more kids out on bikes and playing in their front yards. I thought maybe I could find someone to play with me and Charlie. Down the street to the left I saw something I had never seen before in this neighborhood. It looked like a lemonade stand. I had only seen them on TV and in books. And it was in front of Gavin Eggelston's house.

Gavin used to be a bully to me and the other Number Investigators. But once our teacher Mrs. King assigned me to help him in math class he seemed to be nicer to me. I mean, we're not best friends hanging out all the time, but he's been nicer to me and my friends. I walked Charlie to Gavin's lemonade stand.

"Hi, Charlotte," Gavin waved from behind his stand. His stand was a table, covered in a white table cloth. Two pitchers of lemonade with two stacks of red plastic cups. One stack was large cups and the other stack was small cups.

"Hi, Gavin. A lemonade stand?"

"Yup. I need to earn some extra money. And I fig-ured with it getting warmer and with people riding back and forth on the street with their bikes and with more joggers running, I would be able to make some money."

I read his sign: 50 cents for a lemonade. $1 for an extra-large. That must explain the different sized cups. "How much money have you made so far?" I asked.

"Twelve bucks so far."

"That sounds pretty good. How long have you been out here?"

"About thirty minutes. You want one?"

"I don't have any money. If you've made twelve dollars and you have been out here for thirty minutes you are on pace to make twenty-four dollars per hour."

He reached down underneath the table pulled out a small paper cup. He poured lemonade into the cup and handed it to me. "Try some. Twenty-four dollars per hour you say? Well, you are the one good with numbers."

I took the tiny paper cup of lemonade and drank it. "Actually, that's really good."

"Thanks." He motioned at his sign, "If you want more, it's fifty cents for a regular cup, and one dollar for a large."

"Maybe I'll be back later."

His lemonade gave me an idea.

Chapter 2 $12 on One Package of Cups

"Hey Charlie!" Sally waved from her bike. Charlie jumped at the sound of his name. Sally rode toward us, and she stopped her bike, "Charlotte, did you see Gavin's lemonade stand? Isn't that silly?"

Sally has been my best friend since Kindergarten. We started The Numbers Investigators in the first grade, because our teacher Mrs. Whitlow began math time by going "We're going to investigate numbers today!" So, we went around during recess yelling "We're going to investigate numbers!" and it was there that we began our club. Later, Marcus and Aaron would join.

"Yeah, he told me he has already made twelve dollars," I replied.

Sally paused, "Well, that's not bad, actually."

"The lemonade was actually pretty good," I said.

"You bought some?"

"He gave me a free sample. It's like he knows what he is doing!" I smiled. Charlie jumped up on my leg. "Maybe I need to start a lemonade stand. Charlie here, chewed up one of my mom's shoes. I could help pay it back."

"We could do another business," Sally interrupted.

"Like what?"

Sally paused for a moment, "We could mow lawns."

I shook my head, "That's a terrible idea. Do you even mow your own lawn?"

"Good point! No, I do not."

"I think a lemonade stand just might work. Our only costs would be the lemonade and the cups," I said. "Gavin is charging fifty cents a cup. If there are 24 red cups in a package..."

"He's making twelve dollars on just one package of cups," Sally interrupted.

"And he's charging a dollar for the larger cups," I continued.

Sally was working out the numbers in her head. "And the cost of the lemonade can't be that much per cup. We need to find out how many cups can be made from a package of lemonade. And from there we can find out how much money we could make by multiplying the number of cups per package of lemonade."

"Let's go ask my mom if she has any lemonade. And if she doesn't have any does she know how much a package of lemonade costs and how much it holds," I said.

"I am sure my parents would get us the lemonade for free. Especially if they think I am going to make some money with it." She blew a bubble and let it pop. She was always chewing bubble gum. "Let's meet in the tree house in a few minutes."

"Done," I said. "And let's meet back here after we ask."

Sally ran to her house and I ran into the back door of my house into the kitchen .

"Mom!"

"Yes, Charlotte what is with the shouting?"

"Do we have any lemonade?"

"No. We have water, Coke, and orange juice."

"Ugh!"

"What's the problem?" mom replied.

"Nothing!" and I ran out to the treehouse.

Chapter 3 Refreshing Lemonade

A few minutes later, we met in the tree house.

"Luckily my mom just went grocery shopping," Sally said as climbed into the tree house. Charlie was on the floor chewing his purple ball. "Here is an unopened package of lemonade. She told me to bring it back."

She tossed it to me. The cover said Refreshing Lemonade, there were several lemons on the front with a couple of smiling kids. I read the side of the package, "It says it has sixteen ounces of lemonade mixture and that the package makes sixty-four servings of lemonade."

"How much is a serving?" asked Sally.

"This says a cup," I read the label.

"So, if we charge fifty cents a cup, we will get $32. Because if we charge a dollar a cup we would get $64 and half of $64 is $32," Sally explained.

"$32 for this. And we would need sixty-four cups to be able to sell all of them," I said.

"What are you guys doing?" Aaron's voice shouted from the bottom of the tree.

"We're trying to figure out how to make some money. Come on up," I shouted back.

"Well, if you're trying to make some money I am definitely all in on that," Aaron climbed up the ladder, entered the tree house and sat down on the floor. He was dressed in his baseball uniform. It was clean, so that meant he was going to a game. "So, how are we making money?"

"It seems with a lemonade stand," I replied.

"Yeah, we saw Gavin with a lemonade stand and we thought about the numbers and it seems that we could earn some decent money that way," Sally said.

Aaron furrowed his brow, "Gavin has a lemonade stand? I wonder why he did something like that as opposed to say.... stealing something."

"Stop it," I replied. "He's left us alone."

"But why not mowing lawns or taking dogs for a walk?" Aaron petted Charlie as he said the last part. "You have a dog why don't you walk other people's dogs?"

Sally and I looked at each other.

"I guess we could but listen to the numbers we have been talking about," Sally said. "Gavin is charging 50 cents for a regular size cup and one dollar for a larger cup of lemonade. With those numbers we could sell $32 worth of lemonade from this one package of lemonade mix."

"But you would also have to get the cups. Are your parents going to give all of this stuff to you for free?" asked Aaron

"I am sure they would give it to us," I replied.

"Let's go ask them then," replied Aaron.

And down the ladder we went to go ask my parents.

Chapter 4 We Want to Earn Some Money

"Hey Dad!" I shouted as we entered the kitchen back door.

"Hey Tambourine!" Dad had his head in the refrigerator looking for something to eat.

He calls me Tambourine because when I was two or three I would walk around the house banging a tambourine and the name stuck.

"Can you get us a package of plastic cups."

"What for?"

"We want to do a lemonade stand."

He closed the refrigerator door, "A lemonade stand? What prompted that?"

"Gavin is running a lemonade stand down the street, and he seems to be doing pretty well."

Sally joined in, "And we want to earn some money."

"Certainly nothing wrong with that," Dad replied.

"And when you do earn the money you can pay me back for the shoes Charlie damaged," Mom's voice came from the hallway. She walked in with another shoe. My stomach fell to my knees.

"What's this about?" Dad asked.

"This is the second shoe I have found today that Charlie has chewed up. You missed the first time this morning because you were out on your run. But I am thinking that since Charlie is supposed to be Charlotte's responsibility that she should earn some money for the damage that Charlie has done this morning. Or she should do extra chores around the house to help pay off the debt. And I'm sorry to say that would mean no club meetings and no friends over because Charlotte will be too busy with her extra chores around the house." Mom looked at Sally and Aaron.

"Do they have to go home now? Can we meet and figure out how to earn back the money?" I asked.

"They don't have to go home now, but there definitely can't be any meetings during the week as there has been recently. Figure out how to earn the money either by earning it yourself or by doing a lot of extra chores around the house."

I looked at Charlie who was sitting on his bottom with his head bowed. I think he knew he was in trouble. And now I was in trouble. The Number Investigators would not be meeting until I paid my mom back. Sally and Aaron stood quietly by me.

My dad broke the silence, "So how about this? It shouldn't be that much money to buy you the items for a lemonade stand. But you have to set it up and run it, and you pay your mom off first. Dad looked at Mom, "How much does she owe for the damage?"

"I think $50 is fair. That will allow me to replace one pair of shoes for work."

My head hurt.

Fifty dollars sounded like a lot. We had already calculated $32, but $50 from a lemonade stand? I wasn't sure about that. I nodded my head, "Yes sir, I can do that."

"Well, get in the car. You and I are headed to the grocery store. Sally and Aaron can catch up with you later."

"Yeah, we'll come back later to help you," Sally replied.

"I have to head to my game anyway, I'll come help and bring Marcus with me," said Aaron.

"Let's go, Tambourine," Dad grabbed his keys.

I followed, realizing I was now $50 in the hole, and my friends would soon be banned from the house.

Chapter 5 Shopping with Dad

Dad pushed the grocery cart and looked his list. "Obviously, we need lemonade." He grabbed a large container off the shelf. "This one holds 64 ounces of mix. This will make five gallons of lemonade, let's get two just in case. Each one is $3.99, round that to $4."

"So that's $8 on the lemonade," I said.

"I recommend we get a large cooler with a spout. The kind that people drink from on the sidelines of football and soccer fields."

"How many cups would that hold?"

"I have seen them in five or ten-gallon sizes. There is some math for you, how many cups would that hold?" Dad smiled.

"I'm not sure how many cups are in a gallon."

Dad stopped the cart and explained, "There are four quarts in a gallon. The word quart is related to the word quarter, meaning fourth. There are two pints for every quart..."

"So that means there are eight pints to a gallon," I interrupted.

"Very good! Yes. And there are two cups to every pint..."

"Meaning there are sixteen cups to a gallon," I said.

"There ya go, Tambourine! So, in a five-gallon cooler how many cups would that be?" Dad asked.

I pictured it in my head. Sixteen times five. Six

times five gives me 30. The three tens gets carried. Five times one is five, plus the three gives me 80 . "Eighty cups!" I said. "So, since we have two containers of mix that makes ten gallons that means we can make 160 cups of lemonade with that.

"Excellent! Now let's go find a cooler." He started pushing the cart.

We walked a couple of aisles and turned left. Dad picked up a big one. "Okay, this one holds ten gallons."

"Which means it holds 160 cups," I said.

"Correct, but it costs nearly $50." Dad frowned a little.

My heart sank. I knew that was a lot because of how Dad said the number. And he didn't put the cooler in the cart, he held it above the cart. He was thinking about it. I wasn't sure what to do. Then I saw the numbers in my head. If the cooler held 160 cups, at fifty cents a cup, that would earn $80.

"Dad, if we got that and sold cups at 50 cents each that would earn $80."

"That's true, but the difficulty with this is, we aren't 100% certain that you will sell all the lemonade in the cooler." I wasn't prepared for that thought. He put the cooler back and picked up a smaller one. "This one hold five gallons and it costs $30."

The numbers appeared in my head again. Five gallons is 80 cups. 80 cups at 50 cents each is $40. Still more than the cost of the cooler.

"So how much would you make if we used this

one?" Dad asked.

"40 dollars," I replied. "But since the cooler costs 30 dollars, that would mean I could only make a $10-dollar profit on that cooler."

"Charlotte you're forgetting, that we can always make more lemonade. If we pay $30 for this one, and refill it twice, you would make $80."

"Which would give me a $50 profit!" My mind raced at the untold riches I was about to come into.

"Okay so let's get this cooler and you can pay me back from the revenue you earn at the lemonade stand."

"Revenue?" I cocked an eyebrow at Dad.

"Revenue is the money that is brought in to a business, it is not the profit. Profit as you already seem to know is the money you keep after you have paid all the things that help make the business. In this case, that would be the lemonade mix, the cups, and the cooler. Once your revenue has covered the cost of those items, then your business can be considered profitable. Which, of course, is the whole point of a business."

I smiled my biggest sweetest smile, "You're not getting me the lemonade and cups yourself for free?"

Dad looked at my smile, paused, and replied, "We'll see. Let's go find the cups."

I was certain my smile was going to work. We walked to the other end of the aisle and found the cups. Red and blue plastic cups, one package with smaller cups, and one package with larger cups.

"If your hope is to sell enough lemonade to need to refill it twice, you would need 160 cups. There are 32 cups in each package. If we need 160 cups how many packages do you think we would need to get?"

"That sounds like two-digit division, so I'm not sure," I replied.

"Make a decent guess. How many cups would we have if we had ten packages?"

I saw the numbers in my head. Ten times any number is just that number with a zero attached on the end. "320," I replied.

"We clearly don't need 320 cups..."

"Five packages!" I shouted. "If ten packages gets 320 cups, then five packages would get me 160 cups, because five is half of ten, and 160 is half of 320. So again, five packages needed."

Dad just stared at me for a moment, "That's all correct." He smiled.

"But I think we should get six packages just in case of mistakes," I said.

"Fair enough. Now each package is $5.99, so that's about $36."

$36 for the cups and the $30 for the cooler, that's $66.

I picked up another package of cups, when I saw a larger package. "Dad there are 100 cups in this package, and it's $13.09 a package. With a hundred we would need two packages and the cost would be a little over

$26."

"Well, that's better than the $36 for the other cups." He put the first cups back and picked up two of the large packages of cups.

I started adding the number out loud, "So let's see, that's $26 for the cups, plus the $8 for the lemonade, that's $34. Add the $30 for the lemonade to that and you get $64." Suddenly that sounded like a lot of money for a lemonade stand.

"That sounds about right, Tambourine. Sometimes it costs money to start a business."

Chapter 6 Figuring Out the Profit

"So exactly how much money can we make if we sell all the lemonade you and your Dad bought?" Sally asked. We were sitting on my back porch looking at the lemonade mix, cooler, and cups.

"If we charge 50 cents per cup, we get 80 cups per container of lemonade mix, that gets us $40 per container. And with two packages of lemonade that makes $80."

"But how much did you spend?" Sally asked.

"$66 for everything," I replied.

Sally made a face and I knew what she was thinking, "If your parents made you pay everything back, then that means you would only have fourteen dollars left over. And that's if you sold all the lemonade!"

She was right. I wasn't going to make much money with this approach.

"Hey Charlotte! You back there?" shouted Aaron from the side of the house.

"Yeah, Aaron, we're back here," I replied.

Aaron came around the side, he was dressed in his baseball uniform and he was covered in dirt.

"I see you got all the stuff for the lemonade stand," Aaron sat down and put his baseball glove on the ground.

"We did, but Sally and I were just realizing how little money we would make."

"How much money do you think you would make?" Aaron asked

"Fourteen dollars."

"Wow. That's amazing. At that rate you'll be a millionaire in a thousand years."

"Be quiet," Sally hushed him.

"Hey, are you guys back there?" shouted Marcus from the street.

"Yes, we're back here!" all three of shouted.

Marcus was the fourth member of our Number Investigators club. He joined us last year in the second grade when he moved in from another school.

Marcus ran from the front to the back porch. "What's with all the lemonade stuff?"

"Charlotte needs to earn some money to pay back her mom," Aaron informed him.

Marcus interrupted, "And you saw Gavin doing his lemonade stand and you wanted to do it too."

"How did you know," I asked.

"I just saw him closing up his lemonade stand," Marcus replied.

"Is he still there?" I asked.

"He was thirty seconds ago. Why?" Marcus asked.

"I want to know how well he did." I looked at my three friends, "Let's go ask him before he goes inside!"

18

I ran down the porch steps and my friends followed.

From the driveway I could see Gavin collecting his things from his stand. I ran towards his house. "Hey Gavin! How did you do today?" I shouted.

Gavin waved back. "I did okay."

"How much money did you make, if you don't mind my asking."

"I think about thirty dollars, I haven't counted exactly. Why do you ask?"

"I was just curious," I replied.

Gavin pointed at me, "Wait! You want to do a lemonade stand too!"

I was suddenly so nervous that I laughed, "I need the money."

"You want a new computer or something?"

"I need to pay my mom back for my dog chewing her shoes up, or I get a ton of new chores to do around the house. And while that's happening there can't be a Number Investigators meeting."

"Ha! The great Charlotte Morgan got into trouble!" Gavin grinned.

"Be quiet!" Marcus said.

"Make me!"

I put my hands out, "Stop it! Stop fighting right now you two!" I turned to Gavin, "I didn't mean to get you mad, I just wanted to find out how you did. I need ideas for earning money."

"Well, like I said, I think I made about thirty dollars." I helped Gavin clear off the table and finished stacking the remaining cups.

"How much did the lemonade cost?" asked Sally.

"I don't know. My mom got it. I just used it from the kitchen."

"How many cups did you buy?" Sally kept hounding him with questions.

"I don't know maybe fifty, maybe sixty, maybe a hundred? Again, my mom got this stuff for me."

"You're no help!" Sally huffed.

Gavin stood up and faced Sally. I jumped in, "Thank you for all your help, Gavin! We'll leave you alone now." I handed him the remaining cups.

And we went back to my house.

Chapter 7 Business Ideas

"Well, obviously, you would need to do better than the thirty dollars that he did," said Marcus. We sat in the middle of the tree house.

"I am open to suggestions guys," I replied.

"What about mowing lawns or walking dogs?" Aaron asked.

"I guess I could do that," I said.

"But your parents have already bought the stuff for the lemonade stand remember? Sixty-six dollars' worth of stuff remember?" Sally reminded me. "Let's focus on selling the lemonade first and if we need to earn more we can then do something else."

"Well I guess that means we have to have the greatest lemonade stand ever!" Marcus grinned. "We need to advertise it and let people at school know about it."

"But again, with all the stuff we have even if we sold it all I would make $14," I reminded him.

"What are you charging for a cup of lemonade?" Marcus tilted his head and asked.

"Fifty cents."

"That's too cheap. Go for a dollar a cup."

"Then that gets her only $28, and that's if she sells all the lemonade!" said Aaron.

"So, if we double that cup to two dollars, then that doubles our profit. And $28 doubled is $56," replied Marcus.

"That's getting me closer to what I owe my mom," I replied.

"But that still requires us to sell ALL of the lemonade. And who is going to buy $2 lemonade in a plastic cup from a kid on the street?"

"If people think that it's for a good cause and that Charlotte's lemonade is cool, then people will pay for it," said Marcus.

"Then we need to get people to think Charlotte's lemonade is cool and everyone will want to buy it," Aaron said.

"Selling $2 lemonade sounds very difficult," I replied.

"I think it will beat mowing other people's lawns," responded Sally.

"Good point," I replied.

"I think we need some poster paper and regular paper to create posters and signs for your stand. Gavin didn't have any posters up. He just put his stand out and hoped for the best," Aaron said. "And he seemed to have done okay with that."

Sally raised her hand, "I agree that we need to make posters and signs. I recommend that we meet back here tomorrow afternoon to make some posters for this."

"I am all for making posters," I said.

"Wait!" Aaron interrupted. "Are we still allowed to even be here tomorrow?"

"Yes, but no meetings on school nights," I said.

"Then I guess we better get all our posters done tomorrow," said Sally.

Chapter 8 Dinner

"So, Charlotte, what are your plans for doing the lemonade stand?" Mom asked as she put spaghetti onto my plate. "Can we do it tomorrow since you have all the stuff you need?"

"I want to do it next weekend, not tomorrow. The club wants to make posters and signs to put up," I said.

"That's not a bad idea, wanting to advertise it," Dad replied, his mouth full of bread.

"Where are you thinking about putting posters up?" Mom asked.

"I guess around the neighborhood, like the stop sign on the corner, and the telephone pole where everyone else puts signs up."

"You could put one up here in the front yard. Let everyone know that it will be here," said Dad.

"I would be willing to pass some fliers out at work," Mom replied.

"And I would do the same at school," said Dad.

Mom put down her fork and faced me, "And the other thing is Charlotte you need to be walking Charlie every day. Your father and I can help of course, but Charlie needs to be walked. I think that's why he has been chewing items around the house. He needs to get his energy out. So, I think another expectation is you walk Charlie around the neighborhood every day after school, and not just play with him in the yard. Taking care of a puppy requires making sure his needs are met, and Charlie needs to get his energy out and be trained."

I nodded my head, "Of course, I can do that." And I suddenly realized I could still see my friends during the school week, because I would be out walking the dog. They may not be able to come over here, but there was no rule about not seeing them randomly in the street.

"So, let's come up with a time for this lemonade stand opening," said Dad.

"How about opening at 10 am, that was when Gavin did his."

"Sounds fine to me, no one is going to want to have lemonade too early in the morning. It's not a yard sale. People like yard sales early in the morning, not lemonade," said Mom.

"Now, if you wanted to start a coffee stand, then you would need to start around 6:30 a.m.," smiled Dad.

"Thanks, Dad. Remind me not to start a coffee stand then!"

I now had one week to get ready for the lemonade stand.

Chapter 9 Advertising

At 2:00 pm the next day, Sunday, The Number Investigators met in the tree house.

"What's the date that we are doing this lemonade stand? We need to know what to put on our posters." Sally asked. She had a marker in hand ready to begin writing.

"It's next Saturday, the 21st, at 10 a.m. I talked with my parents last night about when to do this. They also agreed to bring fliers with them to work to pass out."

"Oh, we should totally ask our parents to do the same thing!" shouted Sally. "We can make copies and give them to our parents to give out at work."

Sally drew on her paper and then held it up, and read it out loud, "Saturday April 21st, come and get best lemonade ever! At 23 Willow Run."

"Don't forget to put the time," I said. Sally added it.

Marcus held up his paper and read, "When life gives you lemons make lemonade! Come and get the best lemonade ever next Saturday at 10 am!"

"That sounds sad," Sally said matter-of-factly. "You're advertising that her life is terrible."

"What do you mean?"

"You're saying that Sally's life has given her lemons and now she has to make lemonade, and you want people to drink that?"

Marcus sat silent for a second, "But life did give her lemons. Charlie ate her mom's stuff and she's in trouble."

Sally huffed, "I know that. But you want people to buy the lemonade because it makes them happy, not because Charlotte's in trouble."

Marcus sat dumbfounded. After a moment he responded, "Who died and made you the advertising manager?" He balled up his paper and tossed it into the corner.

Sally motioned with her hands, "Make it happy! Not my life stinks, and now I want you to buy my lemonade! That's all I'm saying!"

Aaron held up his paper, "How about this? Spring is here. It's getting warm. Refresh with the best lemonade. Next Saturday at 10 a.m."

"That's better."

"Don't forget to add the date and the address," I replied.

Sally liked this project and took over, "Let's do this. Everybody works on the regular size sheets of paper. And we will share and come up with the best posters that we should make copies of."

Marcus interrupted, "Also the better ideas, those are the ones that we can put on the large poster paper."

"That's right! Don't touch the poster paper!" Sally spoke over him. "Use the paper as a rough draft, and then we can use the large poster paper as our final copy."

"Final copy? You sound like a teacher," Marcus

grimaced.

"Mrs. King does talk about final copy a lot," She replied, and motioned for us to get to work. For the next fifteen minutes the tree house was quiet as we worked. Pencils, pens, and markers flew across the papers. The tree house floated in an ocean of creativity.

"How about this?" Sally came up for air from her creative dive. "On Saturday, April 21st at 10 a.m. Come experience the best lemonade ever. 23 Willow Run. Don't forget to make a selfie and share!" Sally showed her colorful drawing of two girls smiling with a drink in their hand and taking a selfie. The words were in bright neon pink and yellow. .

Aaron pointed at the girls on the poster, "That's both genius and disturbing all at the same time. Genius because it looks like other advertisements. And disturbing BECAUSE it looks like other advertisements. It's like you memorize advertisements."

"Have you taken a marketing class that I am unaware of?" Marcus inquired.

"We want to make this cool. So that's what appeared in my head when I was thinking about it. Why what did you have?"

For the second time, Marcus balled up his paper and threw it in the corner. "I think I need to try again."

I held up mine. "Saturday the 21st, Charlotte Morgan's Lemonade. Available at 10 a.m."

Sally smiled. "I like that, we can call it Charlotte Morgan's Lemonade. It's a brand!" Her face lit up.

"Or Charlotte's Lemonade," replied Aaron.

"Morgan's Lemonade," said Marcus.

"I like the whole name, Charlotte Morgan's Lemonade," I said.

"I do too. I like the flow," said Sally.

"Here! Let's do this!" Aaron shouted, and he bent over his paper and dove back into his work. We looked over his shoulder. He came back up from the depths of his creativity, "Here's a logo for Charlotte Morgan's Lemonade!"

He showed his drawing. A cup of lemonade with bright beams of sunlight coming out of the cup, and a smiling girl's face, complete with brown pony tail, floated above the cup.

"I like it!" exclaimed Sally, who seemed to be enjoying her new role as the marketing manager of this enterprise. "Let's put that drawing on everything we do!"

"You mean I have to draw this a hundred times?"

"I have a scanner. Make one good copy and then we copy that and print up copies to put on the posters," I said.

Aaron took his time and redrew and colored his illustration. We scanned it on my scanner that I had in my room.

"What are you all up to?" said Dad, popping his head into my room.

The first copy of Aaron's drawing came off the

printer, and I showed it to Dad. "This. Aaron created a label for the lemonade stand, and we're going to put copies of this on all the posters and fliers we make."

Dad looked impressed, "Wow. You have your own brand and everything."

"That's exactly what I said!" Sally gushed.

"Well, I'll leave you hard working entrepreneurs alone." Dad shut the door.

"Entrepreneurs? What's that?" Aaron asked.

"Entrepreneurs are people that start businesses. My dad is one I guess, since he owns his own garage, where they fix cars ," said Marcus.

"Cool, then we are entrepreneurs," said Sally.

"And we have one week until we open for business," said Aaron.

My stomach dropped to floor when he said that. And he was right.

I had one week to get ready for the opening of my lemonade stand.

Chapter 10 Fifteen Posters

The fiftieth copy of Aaron's label came out of the printer.

Sally gave her instructions, "Charlotte we need scissors and tape or glue." I went into my desk and grabbed what she told me to. "So, now that we have these, let's go and finish the posters and put the labels on each one."

Back at the tree house, we dove back into full creative mode. Everyone worked on their own poster, making sure that each one had the address, time, and date. Then we put the label at the top, so it would be visible. When we finished, we had fifteen large posters completed.

"Anyone have any ideas on where to put these?" Sally asked.

"Let's put one on the stop sign at the corner. There's also a telephone pole on the other of the street, where everyone put signs up for yard sales and lost dogs," I pointed in the general direction of where I was thinking.

"But that's only two places. We have fifteen posters, that thirteen more posters we have to hang up," said Aaron.

"I say we go hang these up and if we see any other places, then we put them up there," suggested Marcus.

We left the backyard and headed toward the street. Dad popped his head out of the front door, "Charlotte!

Use this stake and staple gun to help you." I ran up the nineteen steps of the front porch to reach him. "Use this stake in the front yard, tape one of your posters to it. Use the staple gun to attach the posters to any telephone pole you use. Just be careful with it. Do you know how to use it?"

I lied. "Sure!" I took the stake and the staple gun and bounded down the stairs.

"Be careful!" Dad shouted one last time as I ran to the front yard.

I held up the stake, "Look we can use this," I said.

"Are we hunting vampires this afternoon, because I normally think they come out at night, and I need to be home before dark , said Sally."

I rolled my eyes, "Ha! Ha! Very funny. No, we attach a poster to it and place it here in the front yard."

"Good idea. Attach the poster first and then shove it into the ground," instructed Sally.

Marcus taped the poster to the stake and then handed me the sign and stake to me, "It's your yard, you do the honors."

I jammed the stake into the grass and stepped back to view my handiwork. "That looks good. People will definitely know that we will be selling lemonade here."

"You handled that stake well, remind me to call you if I ever do need help with a vampire," said Aaron.

"Thanks for the compliment," I replied.

Armed with the staple gun and a masking tape roll that seemed to weigh five pounds, we headed out to the street. Next on the agenda was taping a poster to the stop sign that was one house to the right of my house.

Sally gave her instructions, "I hope this stays up. Marcus use the masking tape and tape it across the top and bottom."

"Make sure it faces Willow Run. Cars will stop here," Aaron motioned towards Willow Run and where he wanted the poster to face.

"I know that!" Marcus stared at Aaron.

I held the remaining thirteen posters as they did their job. I looked up and down Rosewood Drive, the road that intersected with Willow Run. I pointed to a telephone pole that seemed about a hundred feet away. "I guess we could put one there. There are other posters on it."

Marcus finished taping the poster. He turned and looked. "Okay, but first let's do the one at the other end of Willow Run on the pole near Gavin's house."

The pole was covered in staples from previous posters. Sally and Marcus held the poster. "I'll take the other posters. You use the staple gun, since it's your dad's. I don't want to get into trouble with your parents if I mess it up."

I placed the stapler on the bottom of the poster. I squeezed as hard as I could. But the trigger didn't budge. I squeezed until my face turned red. I used two hands and my face turned red as I struggled with the stapler. I thought I was going to pass out I was struggling so hard with it.

"Wait!" shouted Marcus. "You have the lock on." He stepped away from the poster, took the stapler out of my hand, slid a metal notch from one place to the next, and handed it back to me. "You looked like your head was going to explode. So, I figured I should jump in and help. My dad has one in his garage."

This time, still with some effort though, the staple came out.

"Umm, I can't reach the top of the poster." I stood on my tiptoes and pointed at the top of the poster.

"I got this," grinned Aaron. He got down and all fours, "Use me as a stepladder!"

I stepped on his back, he seemed to wobble a little, but I was able to put a staple in the top of the poster, just above my face in the label. I jumped down off the human stepladder.

"Let's just keep going this way," I pointed towards the intersection with Brown street. We put another poster on the stop sign at that intersection. We next wondered down Brown street and placed two more on telephone poles. After an hour of wondering and placing posters, we went back to my house. We had four posters left.

"There they are!" shouted Dad as he walked out the front door. "Did you put up all your posters?"

Sally held up the four remaining posters, "We have four left, Mr. Morgan."

"Good, then I can take one to school and find a

place to put it," he replied.

"That would be helpful. It would be cool if we got some high schoolers here," said Marcus.

Mom came out the front door as well, "I can take one to work as well."

"I'll give one to my dad and he can have one up at his garage," Marcus took one from Sally.

"Charlotte, take one and see if you can put it at school," Mom suggested.

"That's a good idea," said Sally.

"Okay," I held three of the remaining posters.

Marcus waved, "I'm headed home. I'm tired. I'll you all tomorrow at school."

"We'll catch you later, Charlotte," said Sally and Aaron. They headed back to their houses.

I gave my parents their posters, and I placed one in my room.

I had no idea where I was going to be allowed to hang it at school.

Chapter 11 Poster for Class

"Charlotte, what's with the poster? Did you do a class project?" asked Aniah, a fourth grader.

"No, it's for her lemonade stand that she's going to do next weekend," replied Sally as she walked up to the bus stop.

I pointed to Sally, "What she said."

"Is your teacher going to let you put it up in the classroom?" Aniah asked.

"I don't know. But I guess I will find out."

"Let me see the poster!" yelled Brandon, an energetic second grader. I thought it he was going to rip it as he looked at it. "That's cool looking. It's like you're on a drink bottle." He pointed at Aaron's label.

The other kids at the bus stop looked over my shoulder at the poster. Then most of them walked away.

"I'm sure Mrs. King will let you hang it up in the room," Sally patted my shoulder as the bus pulled up at our stop.

A few minutes later, the bus pulled up at Turing Elementary School. I got off the bus with my backpack and large poster. Luckily, I wasn't the only person walking down the hallway with a large poster. It seemed that several classes had been assigned to bring in a school project on poster board.

At 9:15 a.m. Mrs. King called us to the center of the room onto the carpet for our Morning Meeting. I brought the poster with me. After we greeted each other with a handshake or a high-five to the person sitting next us, Mrs. King went over some announcements for the day, she opened the meeting up for people to share about their weekends. Gavin went biking with his cousin, again. Calvin saw the new comic book movie. Marie went to visit her cousins in Smithville. I never raised my hand.

"Charlotte, aren't you asking to speak? You brought something with you, so I am guessing you have something to share," said Mrs. King.

Sally gave me the thumbs up before I replied. I turned the poster around, so the class could see it. "Sally and I, and a couple of other people made these posters. We went around our neighborhood. We are going to have a lemonade stand at my house next Saturday."

"I wonder where you got that idea!" interrupted Gavin.

"Gavin, please don't interrupt," said Mrs. King using her calm voice. "Charlotte, please continue."

"Yes, I did see Gavin do a lemonade stand this weekend," I continued.

Mrs. King interrupted this time, "Gavin, why didn't you say anything about that, having a lemonade stand? That sounds interesting."

Gavin shrugged his shoulders, "I don't know."

"Anyway Charlotte, I am sorry for interrupting," said Mrs. King.

"That's okay. Gavin did seem to do well with his lemonade stand. And I need to earn some money to pay

37

my mom back for some things, so I thought maybe I could do a lemonade stand."

"Cool," said several students around the room.

"Mrs. King can I keep this poster up in the hallway?" I asked.

Mrs. King paused, "I don't think I can have you put it in the hallway. You're advertising something outside of school. That has nothing to do with school. If you were doing a lemonade stand for the school, then that would be within the rules. But maybe we can hang it here in the room and consider it creative work you have worked on. We can share that here."

"That's fine," I replied. I sat down, and we finished morning meeting. I was hoping the whole school would know about the lemonade stand, but I guess the twenty-four students in Mrs. King's classroom would have to be enough for now. I had six days until the lemonade stand, I was going to have to figure another way for more people to know about it.

Six days.

Chapter 12 Six Days

I got off the school bus and headed for home. Mom was waiting at the door with Charlie and his leash. "Remember our deal. You need to walk him and train him." Charlie looked like he was going to throw his back out as he wagged his tail.

"Okay," I replied. I tossed my backpack on the ground, grabbed Charlie, his leash, and a bag to clean up after him, and bolted out the front door. Charlie only walked a few steps before he relieved himself.

"You stole my idea!" Gavin shouted from down the street. He got on his bike and began riding towards me. I waved at him.

"You're not mad, are you? I thought it was good idea. And I owe my mom some money for my dog chewing up her shoes."

He stopped his bike a few feet from me. He smiled, "I'm just messin' with you. Maybe we should start a competition. I can run a lemonade stand that weekend as well, and let's see who earns more money!" He grinned from ear to ear. My stomach felt nauseated, I didn't want to compete with him. I didn't need that sort of stress, and he might take away from the people that come to buy lemonade from me! "Relax! I'm not going to set up another stand." I let out my breath. "I could see it on your face, relax, I'm just teasing you."

"It wasn't funny. I need that money."

"Alright! Alright! Alright! I get it. So, he chewed up some of your mom's stuff?" He pointed at Charlie who was busy investigating the grass with his nose.

Something had been there to get his attention.

"Yeah, I have to replace a pair of her shoes. I need to make a profit around $50."

"That would be a good haul. I only got about $34 from mine."

"Did you have to pay your parents back for the lemonade?" I asked.

"No. Why would I do that? I just used the lemonade that we already had in the kitchen."

I shook my head, "I'm just curious."

I turned around to continue my walk with Charlie. And for whatever reason Gavin decided to follow me. Charlie was difficult to walk on the leash, as he kept wanting to follow Gavin on his bike. I reached the end of the street and turned right onto Rosewood Drive. Charlie still had not done his business, so I kept walking.

"Hey Charlotte!" shouted Sally. She ran out of the front door of her house. I stopped and waited for her. She ran up to us. I could tell by the look on her face she was wondering why Gavin was with me. "I'm allowed to hang out with you while you walk Charlie, that's not against the rules?"

"It's fine. Just no coming over."

"Wait! You're grounded," Gavin pointed at me.

"The Number Investigators can't come over during the week until I pay my mom back."

"Yeah, you're grounded," he replied.

"So, what if I'm grounded?" I asked Sally.

"Who knows what he is thinking." she replied.

"I'm just saying that Charlotte Morgan is never in trouble!" Gavin said.

"Yeah, that ain't true," I replied.

"I never see you get into trouble at school," he shot back.

"That doesn't mean anything. I still get into trouble at home."

"Okay, fine. It's just nice to know that even Charlotte Morgan gets into trouble once in a while. You're not so perfect."

I was stunned. Someone thought I was perfect.

"It doesn't matter. What matters is that I have to find a way to pay my mom back, and we have bought all the materials to do a lemonade stand, and we made all the posters to advertise it." I pointed at a poster that was still on the telephone pole.

Gavin looked impressed, "That's cool."

I kept walking, Sally and Gavin followed.

"Where else did you put up signs?" he asked.

Sally made a circular motion with her index finger, "We hung posters all around the neighborhood."

"That's why you wanted to hang that one at school," Gavin replied. "I guess you could have a lot of people come to your lemonade stand. What happens if you have too many people and they can't fit on the street?"

I looked at Sally, and I shrugged my shoulders, "I don't know."

"I think that would be a wonderful problem to have," Sally said. "I think the real problem would be having no one come to see us."

Charlie stopped and did his business.

"Yeww!" moaned Gavin.

I rolled my eyes as I picked up Charlie's poop with the bag. "What are you? Four?"

"Are you going to be helpful or not?" said Sally, clearly exasperated with Gavin.

"Okay! Okay! I'll stop. If you want me to help with the lemonade stand I can."

"How?" I asked.

"Umm...I can make lemonade popsicles ."

Sally and I looked at each other.

"Lemonade popsicles? That's actually not a bad idea," said Sally. "Instead of using all the lemonade to make drinks. We could use some of it to make popsicles."

"And we could charge more for the popsicles!" I said. "That's a good idea Gavin! But we don't need you to make the Popsicles. I already have the stuff."

"Actually, now we would need to get the sticks for

the Popsicles," Sally informed me.

"I got the idea when someone at my stand said I should do it. It was hot enough for them to ask for something even colder. And I was like 'I don't have time to do that, too!' I told them."

"That's wonderful customer service Gavin," replied Sally. "Remind me to not have you behind the table at our stand."

"Whatever! If you need my help, you know where to find me," He waved off Sally, turned around, and rode his bike back to his house.

"This Popsicle idea is very good," I said once he left.

"I know. But he was being a pain. We could charge several dollars for each popsicle. And I think we could get more popsicles out of the lemonade mix than we would drinks."

"We could do really well with popsicles," I said. "Now, I just need to know how to make them. And I need to do it without the rest of the Number Investigators."

"Here's a plan. You walk Charlie every day after school around the block, and we will have a Number Investigators meeting as you walk Charlie. And we'll do the math together," Sally smiled at her thought.

"I'm good with that."

I now had less than six days to get ready for the lemonade stand. And now I had to figure out how to sell popsicles as well.

Chapter 13 Gavin's Idea

"Sally and I decided that we can meet after school while I walk Charlie," I said to Aaron and Marcus as we walked the track at the beginning of recess.

"That's cool." Aaron replied.

"Did you tell them about Gavin's idea?" Sally asked.

"What idea?" Marcus asked.

"Gavin said that someone asked for popsicles when he did his lemonade stand," I replied. "And I thought maybe if we did that we could charge more for each frozen lemonade."

Aaron clapped his hands, "Yeah! You could charge like $5. That would be a great mark-up!" Aaron stared off into space, apparently imagining great riches.

Sally interrupted his fantasy, "But the question becomes, how much does it cost to make a frozen lemonade?"

Aaron shrugged his shoulders, "I don't know? What do we need? Wooden popsicles sticks..."

"Molds, the things that hold the lemonade..." interrupted Marcus.

"And a cooler with ice to be able to keep them frozen," I said, as I imagined going through all the steps that were needed.

"So that's a cooler, ice, popsicles sticks, and molds," said Sally, who seemed to be keeping a list in her head. "That sounds like a lot. Maybe charging even $5 might not be enough."

"It will depend on how much all that stuff costs," said Marcus.

"How are we going to get all of this stuff?" Aaron wondered.

"I don't know," I replied. "I don't know."

"A bag of ice can't be more than a dollar, and if we get three..." said Aaron.

"Then that's three bucks," replied Sally.

"Do you have cooler?" asked Aaron.

"Yes! We do! We use it when we go to the beach, and we put our snacks in it!" I yelled because I was excited to know that was one less expense.

"What about the things to make popsicles, the holder thingies," Aaron pretend to hold a popsicles and pull it out of the holder.

"I think their called molds, since they make the shape of the popsicle," I replied.

"Yeah, that. How much are those? Do you have any?" Aaron asked.

"I have one. I think it makes six," I replied.

"Well, that's not enough!" Aaron replied.

"Clearly that wouldn't be enough. But I would need to get more," I said.

"Hey!" Gavin shouted from the monkey bars in middle of the of the track. He and Calvin always sprinted their lap around the track, so he was always finished first and went to playing on the monkey bars before anyone else.

"Why does he do that? Why doesn't he just come up here and talk to us?" Sally wonder aloud.

"What!" I shouted back. "Come up here if you want to talk to us! We're clearly still walking our lap!"

Gavin jumped down off the monkey bars and Calvin followed him.

"Are you guys talking about your lemonade stand?" Gavin asked.

"Yeah, so what?" replied Marcus. Marcus still didn't trust Gavin, he thought that Gavin was still going to bully us for being The Number Investigators.

"Hey look! I am just trying to be nice. I was just wondering if you guys had come up with any other ideas for your stand?" Gavin replied.

"I told them about the idea of the popsicles of frozen lemonade you told me about yesterday," I said.

"You could just buy frozen popsicles and resell them," Gavin said.

"Why would people buy things more expensively from us that they can get at the grocery store for less?" asked Aaron.

"I don't know. I'm just giving out ideas."

Calvin joined in the conversation, "What about baking cookies and selling those?"

I rolled my eyes, "Y'all are making this more complicated than it needs to be. I don't have time to make cookies."

"Ask your parents to make them," suggested Gavin.

"My parents would kill me if I asked them to bake cookies, especially since the point of all of this is to pay my mom back."

Chapter 14 Frozen Lemonade

As soon as I walked in the back door from school, I threw my backpack into the corner and began rummaging through the freezer.

"Tambourine! What are you doing?" Dad asked.

I looked out from behind the freezer door. "I am looking for those things we use to make Popsicles during the summer. They're blue and have six compartments with a plastic stick that goes in them."

"I know what you are talking about. Why are you looking for them?"

"Sally and I had thought if we sold frozen lemonade we could make more money than with just drinks. Gavin gave us the idea."

Dad reached into the freezer and moved some frozen pizzas and pulled out the Popsicles molds I was looking for.

"This holds six," he held them up.

"I can count to six Dad."

"Then you should know that you can't make any money with just six. Plus, these are plastic and fit into molds, and they go with the mold. If we give these away with the frozen lemonade we wouldn't have the holders anymore. If you want to sell frozen lemonade, we need to think of a way to use regular wooden Popsicles sticks. And we would need a way to make more than six," said Dad. "Here, I'll take you to the store after you finish walking Charlie."

I shut the freezer door, grabbed Charlie's leash, a bag, and took Charlie outside.

I managed to get to the street in front of the house before Sally saw me. She bolted out her front door and met me on the street.

"My dad is going to take me to the store after I walk Charlie to see about getting stuff to make the frozen lemonade popsicles," I said.

"That's cool," Sally replied.

"Hey! Charlotte! Sally!" It was Aaron running up from his house, and one of the few times I didn't see him in some sort of sports uniform. He was wearing a New York Yankees t-shirt though. "You all talking about the lemonade stand?"

"I just told Sally that my dad wants to take me to the store after I finish walking Charlie so we can get things to make frozen lemonade."

"Where are you going to freeze them? How many are you going to need?" Aaron asked.

"I don't know. How many do you think I am going to need? I've never done this before."

"If you charge $5 per frozen lemonade, you would only need to sell ten to make your $50," said Aaron.

"But that would be $50 in revenue, not in profit. I have no idea how much the stuff is to make the frozen lemonade!" I replied.

"Well hopefully it won't be much," he replied.

"Isn't $5 a little much for a frozen lemonade?" Sally asked.

"People will think it's fancy frozen lemonade!" Aaron smiled. "You can't buy Charlotte's frozen lemonade in stores. WE CAN ADD THAT TO A POSTER!" Aaron made a sweeping gesture with his hands, "Not Available in Stores!" He his face lit up like the Fourth of July.

Charlie did his business, and I cleaned it up. "Come on Charlie, let's go home and get Dad to take us to the store!" I turned to Sally and Aaron, "Sorry to cut our meeting short, but I am headed to the store!"

"Catch you later!" replied Sally and Aaron.

I tossed Charlie's bag into the outside trashcan and bounded into the back door and into the kitchen.

"Let's go Dad!"

He was already with his keys waiting for me, "Let's go shopping, Tambourine!"

Chapter 15 $111 in Supplies

We turned down the aisle in the grocery store. The molds for the Popsicles were on the aisle with all the summer stuff. "Okay, here's a set," said Dad, he picked up a set. It was made of a silver metal, and it came with a metal rack to hold it. It made ten Popsicles. He pulled up another one, it was purple, made of plastic, it only made six Popsicles at a time.

"Okay," Dad said, looking at the silver one, "this one costs a lot, $39.99."

"So, $40," I replied. "That means it would cost $4 for each frozen lemonade I made."

"This one is less expensive," holding up the plastic purple set. "It only costs $4.99"

"So, $5 for that one. Which means I that each frozen lemonade would cost less than a dollar to make. Six popsicles for five dollars. So, let's get that one."

Dad shook his head, "That math only works for the first batch you make. If you made the popsicles and then kept them frozen in the cooler. You could make several more. So, for the silver one, yes, it costs more, but you would freeze them and then keep the extras in a cooler or the freezer. Of course, you could get the purple plastic one..."

"But then I could only make six at a time. With the other one I could make ten at a time. I could make more at once."

Dad held up both. He wasn't going to tell me which one to get.

"Get the metal one, it's more expensive, but with the ability to make more at once, I can get more to sell faster." I pointed at the holder, "Also I like the holder, and this one seems to be designed to hold the wooden sticks. The plastic one comes with its own plastic handles."

Dad put the silver one into the cart, "Good decision. Now what else do you think we will need?"

"Wooden popsicles sticks obviously," I said.

"You're also going to need some plastic sandwich bags to hold the popsicles after they're frozen. We'll place them in our picnic cooler with ice and then just pull them out of the cooler when you sell one."

"I never would have thought of that!"

"Glad I can help."

The cost of the metal molds was $39.99, the popsicle sticks was $1.99, and the lunch bags was 99 cents. Which totaled $42.97, add the five percent sales tax, and the grand total was $45.12.

Round that to $45 and add the $66 for the cooler and lemonade, and cups, and now we had spent was $111.

This was getting more expensive by the day.

The numbers appeared in my head, I was going to need to sell over $160 worth of lemonade and frozen lemonade to make enough proof to pay Mom back.

One hundred and sixty dollars in sales.

I had five days to prepare.

I was terrified.

Chapter 16 No One is Going to Go to Your Stand

I got off the bus and walked into school. It was Wednesday morning.

"Hey Charlotte! I heard about your lemonade stand! I'll come by Saturday and check it out," shouted Kevin Kershner, a fifth grader that lived one street over on Den Bark Drive.

I waved to him, "How did you know about it?"

"I saw the posters you put around the neighborhood! I'll catch you later," and he headed off to class. I stood in the middle of the hallway as students walked around me.

"Charlotte! You're doing a lemonade stand?" asked Leigh Brackett, she was a fourth grader in Mr. Martin's class.

"Umm....yeah..."

"Cool, I'll try and make it! Have a good one!"

"Wait Leigh! Who told you about the lemonade stand?"

"Umm...a couple of other people told me about it. And I saw your posters in the neighborhood. The posters looked cool. I'll catch you later!" She waved at me as she headed to Mr. Martin's class.

"Charlotte! Stop standing in the middle of the hallway and come to class!" said Mrs. King from the classroom doorway. I came back to earth and headed to class.

Three hours later at lunch, I sat down with Sally, Aaron, and Marcus. "I had two people tell me this morning that they were coming to the lemonade stand on Saturday!"

"Who?" replied Sally.

"Kevin in fifth grade, he lives over on Den Bark, and Leigh, in Mr. Martin's class told me."

"When did they tell you?" asked Marcus.

"This morning in the hallway as we were coming to class. In fact, Leigh told me that other people had told her about it. But both she and Kevin had told me that they had seen the posters."

Marcus grinned, "That means those posters worked! And it sounds like we are going to have a successful lemonade stand this weekend." He rubbed his hands together.

Sally patted me on the back, "Yeah, Charlotte this might actually work."

"Hey Charlotte!" yelled Brian Kirkland from the table behind me, a third grader in Mrs. Raven's class, "A lemonade stand? Good luck, I don't think it's going to work!"

"Brain turn around, no yelling across the tables," said Mrs. Ritchie, a lunchroom monitor.

"What was that about?" said Marcus. "I am going to deal with him during recess." He pointed at Brian's back, but Brian wasn't looking at him. "At recess pal!"

"Let it go, Marcus," I said.

Mrs. Ritchie walked past the table and over to the Kindergartners. Brian turned back around, "No one is going to your lemonade stand," he put air quotes around the words lemonade stand.

Marcus got mad. He wanted to stand up. He looked around for Mrs. Ritchie. "Why would he say that. What is his problem?"

"Sit down before you fall down!" said Aaron in a silly accent as he pointed to Marcus's seat. Marcus sat down.

Suddenly I was uncomfortable that my lemonade stand was popular enough to have people fight over it.

Chapter 17 Where's Brian?

"Is Brian out here yet?" Marcus looked around the playground as we walked the track at the start of recess.

"Please don't get something started and then get us into trouble," pleaded Sally.

"Let's just be thankful that other people said that they are going to come," I replied.

"Maybe if he comes, I can shove a frozen lemonade down his throat!" Marcus exclaimed.

"Hey Charlotte!" Gavin came running up to us. Like normal he had already finished his lap. "I hear a lot of people are going to come to your lemonade stand on Saturday."

"Thanks Gavin. I've had a couple of others tell me the same thing."

"Have you seen Brian?" Marcus asked.

"Kirkland?" Gavin turned and pointed at the class heading onto the track. "He must be over there in his class. Why?"

"He called the lemonade stand stupid!" Marcus replied. He got madder the more he talked about it.

"He didn't call it stupid." I said.

"He put air quotes around it," Marcus replied. "There he is!" He pointed at Brian and headed toward him, the rest of us followed along wondering what was about to happen.

"Marcus, what are you going to do?" asked Sally.

"You'll see." Marcus clenched his fists. "Brian! What was that you were talking about during lunch? Why is our lemonade stand stupid?" Marcus was seething. I wasn't sure what was about to happen.

"I didn't say the lemonade stand was stupid!" Brian shouted back. "I just don't think anyone is going to come to it!"

Marcus took a step forward. Aaron put his shoulder on Marcus in an attempt to keep him from jumping on Brian. "Why!" shouted Marcus.

I saw Mrs. King look at us, "Marcus, tone it down."

"It is going to rain on Saturday!" said Brian. My heart sank. "That's why I said no one was coming to the lemonade stand on Saturday."

Marcus stood not saying anything. After a tense moment he broke his silence, "Why didn't you say that?"

"Because Mrs. Ritchie was watching us. I would have thought that you guys knew that it was supposed to rain this weekend?" Brian looked at all of us.

"No one has told us that," I replied.

"Just ask your parents when you get home. I have a game this weekend. My parents told me that it may get rained out."

Brian went to jog his lap around the track, and my heart was in my stomach.

Chapter 18 Mom is it going to rain?

"Mom is it going to rain?" I shouted as I busted into the back door. I threw my backpack in the corner. Charlie ran up under my feet.

"Charlotte, why are you yelling?" Mom asked.

"A boy at school said it was supposed to rain this Saturday!"

Mom made a face, then pulled out her phone, made a few swipes and began to read, "There is a 60% chance of rain on Saturday." Mom made a face, "It may rain Charlotte, but it is April and there is more rain during this time of the year. Remember the phrase April Showers Bring May Flowers."

"Then what am I going to do if it rains?"

"Well let's just wait and see until Saturday before we begin panicking. It's Wednesday, so there is time for the forecast may change, but if it does, you can always just do it the next weekend."

"Ugh!" I exclaimed.

"There's no need to get upset Charlotte. But it's not raining now, so you can go and walk Charlie."

Chapter 19 Friday

I got off the bus and ran into the back door. Charlie was waiting for me at the door. His whole body wagged back and forth as he ran up underneath me. I threw my backpack into the corner.

I went to the freezer. I pulled out the ten frozen Popsicles, put them into bags placed them in the bottom of the freezer. I poured lemonade into the ten molds and placed the molds back into the freezer.

Charlie stood close behind me, his tail wagging his whole body back and forth.

I grabbed Charlie's leash and bag. I put his leash on him, and we went out the door.

Sally, Marcus, and Aaron were already waiting for me outside at the street.

"So, what else is there to do?" Aaron asked. They followed me as I walked Charlie.

"Have you finished freezing the Popsicles?" Sally asked.

"I'll have forty ready after the ten I just put in the freezer," I replied.

Marcus rubbed his hands together, "You'll do really well if you sell all of those. At five dollars a piece with forty of them, you'll make two hundred dollars on those alone!"

I smiled, "I know. I am glad we decided to do them. And since it only costs forty dollars for the mold, that'll bring a profit of about $160. You know minus the cost of the lemonade and the popsicle sticks. Which isn't much."

"So closer to $150 then," replied Sally.

"Yes, closer to $150, thanks for reminding me to round," I said.

"If you sell everything, you will make $150 on the frozen lemonade, and $50 from the lemonade, so that makes $200," said Aaron. "That sounds pretty good to me!"

"But, in order for that to happen, I have to sell everything. Everything!"

"That's true, but it gives you some room to still make a $50 profit and pay your mom back," said Sally,

"And that's what I need to do," I replied.

There was now only eighteen hours until I opened the lemonade stand—1080 minutes or 64,800 seconds.

Chapter 20 The Lemonade Stand

My alarm went off at 7:30 a.m., but I was already wake. I had had a dream about no one coming to my lemonade stand. I shook my head, rubbed my hands over my face, brushed my hair, got dressed and headed downstairs.

"Good morning, Tambourine!" Mom and Dad were drinking their coffee at the kitchen table. "The usual?" he asked.

"Yes! Pancakes please," I responded.

Dad scrolled through his phone, "It looks like the rain may not get to us today. It looks like the clouds will break up around 10:30 this morning."

"That's some good news. I hope it's true."

I finished the pancakes, complete with syrup and blueberries. "Well, I'm ready to try and sell some lemonade!"

"Well, let's go!" Dad clapped his hands. Mom and Dad stood up from the table.

The doorbell rang.

"Who is that at this time in the morning?" my mother wondered. She looked out the front window, "Charlotte it's your friends."

The Number Investigators were at the door, Sally, Marcus, and Aaron were waiting with smiles on their faces.

Dad put up the table. Mom brought out the cups

and napkins. Aaron and I mixed the first container of lemonade. Sally and Marcus put the Popsicles into the cooler. But the time we were ready it was 9:45 a.m.

At 9:51 a.m. our first customer showed up.

It was Gavin.

He stood in front of my table, put his finger to his chin as if he was thinking, and then hummed, "Hmmm... Hmmm...." He kept tapping his finger to his cheek. "What do I want...What do I want..." he said over and over.

I gave him a look.

He furrowed his brow and pointed at the sign hanging from my stand, "Can I have a lemonade?" he asked.

"That's will be one dollar please," I said.

Gavin handed me four quarters. One quarter is twenty-five cents, so four makes four quarters . Dad took a picture of Gavin handing me the money.

"Dad!" I shouted. I was so embarrassed.

Gavin took a sip of the lemonade. "Wow! That is good. I'll take another!"

"Gavin you don't have to do that!" I said.

"Take the boy's money!" shouted Sally.

Gavin gave me another four quarters, and I made another lemonade.

A red car drove up and parked on the street in

front of the house.Mrs. King got out of the car—my teacher! I rarely ever see teachers outside of school. I once saw my Kindergarten teacher pushing her baby in a stroller at the grocery store, but I certainly have never had a teacher come to my house. Mrs. King was dressed in shorts, a t-shirt, and bright pink running shoes. Running shoes—I wonder if Mrs. King actually runs. I noticed that she didn't have pencil hidden behind her ear. I guess there was no need for pencils on a Saturday.

"Mrs. King! What are you doing here?" I said.

"I wanted to try the greatest lemonade ever made!" she said. "And I would like a frozen lemonade as well please."

"That will be six dollars please," I said. I couldn't believe my teacher was handing me money. Sally, Marcus, and Aaron just stood silently, they seemed to be in disbelief that a teacher was standing in my front yard. Mrs. King first took a bite of the frozen lemonade, and then took a drink. Mrs. King handed me a five-dollar bill and a one-dollar bill , "Here is ten dollars."

I reached into the money drawer. I knew that I owed Mrs. King four dollars. I pulled out four one-dollar bills, "Here is your change, four dollars."

Mrs. King put up her hand, "Charlotte, keep the change."

"Oh, please it's four dollars, take the change," I wasn't sure what to do. I looked at Dad.

"Thank you, Mrs. King," said Dad.

"I insist," she replied.

"Thank you," I put the two quarters back into the money drawer.

"Charlotte, this is great! You are going to do very well today, especially since the rain is going to hold off and it is going to be warm today!" She finished her lemonade and ate her frozen lemonade. She waved, got into her car and drove off.

"Your teacher came to your house," said Marcus.

"And she gave you money!" said Aaron. "Your teacher gave you money."

"Charlotte! Charlotte!" shouted Maggie Winchester. She was a four-year-old who lived two doors down. She was out in her front yard. Her mother was with her, and they walked over.

"Charlotte! Charlotte! I want a lemonade!" She bounced up and down. She held out a dollar bill to me. I gave her lemonade, and her twoquarters in change. She chugged the lemonade, "Mmmm...that's good!"

"Thank you, Charlotte," said Mrs. Winchester. "I hope you do well today! Come on Maggie, let's get out of Charlotte's way."

"Okay, let's go grab our signs and go stand at the stop sign to get people's attention," instructed Sally. She passed out the signs and they headed for the corner of Willow Run and Rosewood. They held their signs up and jumped up and down as cards passed by.

After the Winchesters went back to their house more people who lived on Willow Run wandered out and came over to visit me and buy lemonade. The clouds slowly went away, and the day became brighter.

A line grew at the stand.

Little Mickey, a two-year-old that live at the far of the street, walked to me with money in his hand that his mother had given him. "I wanta wemonade!" He was so cute as he walked up to me and handed me the money.

"Of course, you can have a lemonade!" I replied.

I handed him the cup slowly. "Fank you!" he replied. His mom waved and smiled at me. He walked back to his mom.

The line grew. And it grew so much that Aaron, Sally, and Marcus put down their signs and came to help.

For the next hour, I never sat down.

"We are about to run out of lemonade!" said Aaron.

"Don't panic, come with me and help me make some more," said Dad, and they took a cooler and went inside.

"How are we doing on popsicles?" Sally asked as she opened to cooler. "It looks like we have about twenty left."

"Then shut the cooler, we don't want them melting," I replied.

At 10:45 am the sky was clear, and the clouds had gone away. The line grew shorter. Kids that had bought lemonade and popsicles were still hanging around. Some were riding bikes, they carried their cups of lemonade in their mouth. Others played tag up and down the street.

At 11:00 kids were still hanging around and playing. But the line was much shorter.

Mrs. Smith and her son Michael, who lived one street over, handed me some money. "Two popsicles and a two lemonades please."

"That will be twelve dollars," I replied.

Mrs. Smith handed me the money, and Sally got the popsicles. "Well, you got the two last popsicles." She pulled them out and gave them to Michael and his mom.

My dad tilted the cooler and finished filling the cups with lemonade. "You also seemed to have gotten the last of the lemonade," He handed them the cups.

"Wow! That is lucky! You seemed to have done very well today Charlotte!" said Mrs. Smith.

"It's been very busy for the last hour, so yeah it looks like I did do well. Thank you for coming!"

"Are we really completely out of lemonade and popsicles?" asked Marcus.

"It seems that we are!" I replied.

"Then let's put this sign up!" smiled Marcus. The sign had the word "CLOSED" scrawled across it.

"Now, let's count some money!" grinned Marcus as he rubbed his hands together.

Dad gave us our instructions, "Okay! I know you want to go and do that. Go count the money and then get back out here and I'll help you take everything down.

So, count your money quickly."

"Yes! To the tree house!" I said, and we ran to the tree house.

Chapter 21 Counting Money!

The four of us sat down in a circle in the tree house. I put the money box in the middle.

I pulled out the bills and made sure they were sorted with the correct dominations, tens with tens, fives with fives, and ones with ones.

I handed the coins to Sally, "You count the change, they seem to be all quarters." Four quarters equals one dollar.

I started counting the ten dollars bills first—twenty-one. Twenty-one ten-dollar bills equals 210 dollars. Two hundred and ten!

"I am already starting with $210!" I shouted.

"That is awesome!" exclaimed Aaron.

"Shh!!!" scolded Sally as she sorted the quarters into groups of four.

I counted the five dollar bills next, there were twenty. Twenty five-dollar bills equals one hundred dollars. Wow!

I don't think I ever had a hundred dollars before, much less the three-hundred and ten dollars I had now.

I picked up the one-dollar bills and counted. Forty one-dollar bills.

"Okay, so I have forty one-dollar bills, that brings me to a grand total of $350. Have you finished counting the quarters?" Sally had the quarters all stacked in well placed stacks of four quarters each.

"There are fifty-six quarters, which means you have fourteen dollars in quarters," said Sally, she motioned with pride at her impeccable stack of quarters.

Aaron raised his hand, "Wait, that brings the total to $364. That's one more dollar than everything we counted on if we sold everything. Did you miss count?"

"If she is only off by four dollars, what difference does it make?" asked Marcus.

"We're the Number Investigators!" Aaron replied, and Marcus understood.

"Wait a minute! Mrs. King, let me keep the change. And that was four dollars! That's the difference!"

"She's right. Mrs. King did give her the extra change," replied Sally.

"How much do you owe your mom again?" Marcus asked.

"She said fifty dollars."

"$360 minus $50 means a profit of $310!" said Aaron. "Three hundred and ten dollars!" His face lit up like a Christmas tree.

"I have to pay my dad back for the stuff he bought," I said. "There's more to this than the total number of dollars we brought in. He said that it was a total of $111."

The tree house got quiet.

"That's a lot," Marcus said.

"It takes money to run a business," I replied. I did

the numbers in my head, "That brings the total down to $199."

"That's a lot!" said Aaron. "You made nearly $200 this morning."

"Well, I need to split it between us," I said. "I mean we did this all together. You helped with the posters and with selling today. So, we need to split this four ways."

"What's $199 divided by four?" Sally asked.

"Well, $200 divided by four is $50," I said. "And since $199 is one dollar less, split between the four of us."

Aaron interrupted, "So one dollar divided by four is twenty-five cents less for each of us, making it $49.75 we each get."

"Yes," I said.

"And we got plenty of quarters for the seventy-five cents," Sally motioned to the quarters in front of her.

"I need to pay my mom and dad first before we get our split. Let's go give them their money," I said, and we headed down out the tree house and to the house.

Chapter 22 The Profit

"Hey Mom, Dad," I shouted as we bounded into the kitchen. Dad was wiping out the cooler that held the frozen popsicles, and Mom held the lemonade cooler upside down in the sink.

"Yes! Charlotte!" Dad yelled, he likes to yell back at me when I talk too loudly in the house.

"We made $364!"

"Charlotte, that's wonderful!" my mom smiled. "That's excellent!"

I put the money on the counter. "How much do I owe you again for the shoes?"

"I said fifty dollars would cover it."

I counted out five ten-dollar bills, "Here you go. I am sorry about Charlie again."

"Thank you, sweetie."

"And Dad, the total you spent on everything was $111 correct?" I looked at him.

He looked at me and nodded, "Yes, it was."

I counted out eleven ten-dollar bills to make $110 and a dollar bill to make $111. I handed it to Dad. "Here you go."

He looked at the money. "I am very impressed, Tambourine."

"Can we go to back to the tree house, so we can split the remaining money?" I asked.

Mom nodded, "Yes, Charlotte, you guys go ahead and play. We'll finish up here. You did a great job today."

"Thanks, Mom."

We ran back to the tree house.

I sat down on the floor and called us into a meeting, "Here Ye! Here Ye! Let this meeting of The Number Investigators come to order!"

"You're very loud when you do that!" said Aaron.

"I know," I grinned.

"I recommend that this special meeting is to split the remaining profit from today's lemonade stand."

"Seconded!" shouted Sally.

And with that we split the remaining $199 among ourselves.

"Not a bad way to spend a Saturday," said Marcus.

"Now, let's just make sure that Charlotte trains Charlie so we don't have to do this every weekend!" declared Sally.

"Good point," I said. "I guess I better go do that now."

"Let's go help her," said Aaron.

We went inside. I put away my $49.75 into a drawer.

My friends, The Number Investigators, then helped

me walk Charlie.

About the Author

Martin Tiller taught elementary school for twelve years.

He lives in Virginia with his daughter, and a dog names Leia.

He has written ten other books:

<u>The Kevin Books Series:</u>

Kevin and the Seven Lions

Kevin and the Three-Headed Alien

Kevin and the Triple Creature Feature

<u>The Dolbin School series:</u>

Dolbin School for the Extraordinary

The Dark Cloud Rises

The Return of the Professor

Finals

<u>The Number Investigators series:</u>

Charlotte Morgan and the Great Big Math Problem

Other books:

Baseball and Aliens

Irving Williams and the Mystery of the Lighthouse Ghost

Martin can be found online at:

martintiller.com

Please visit and leave a note.

Made in United States
Troutdale, OR
06/15/2024

20505372R10046